D0967507

For Rory Anderson,
who listened to me telling stories
on October 13, 2008
S.G.

For Betty
J.B.

ORCHARD BOOKS
338 Euston Road, London NW1 3BH
Orchard Books Australia
Hachette Children's Books
Level 17/207 Kent Street, Sydney NSW 2000

First published in the UK in 2009
First paperback publication in 2010

Text © Sally Grindley 2009
Illustrations © Jo Brown 2009

The rights of Sally Grindley to be identified as the author and
Jo Brown to be identified as the illustrator of this work
have been asserted by them in accordance with the
Copyright, Designs and Patents Act, 1988.

A CIP catalogue record for this book is available from the British Library.
All rights reserved.

ISBN 978 1 84616 156 8 (hardback)
ISBN 978 1 84616 164 3 (paperback)

1 3 5 7 9 10 8 6 4 2 (hardback)
1 3 5 7 9 10 8 6 4 2 (paperback)

Printed in China

Orchard Books is a division of Hachette Children's Books,
an Hachette UK company.

www.hachette.co.uk

The Strange Pawprint

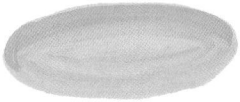

Written by SALLY GRINDLEY
Illustrated by JO BROWN

ORCHARD BOOKS

Constable Tiggs
Sergeant Bumble
Albert

One cold, snowy morning, the Bear Detectives were woken by a loud knocking.

"Wake up! Wake up!" somebody shouted.

Constable Tiggs
leapt out of his
bed and ran
downstairs.

He found Albert, the repair-bear, on the doorstep. "What on earth has happened?" he said, shivering.

"I was checking the ground for holes, which is difficult in all this snow, when I found a strange pawprint," said Albert.

"What sort of strange?" asked Tiggs. "It looks as if the thing that made it has no fur, no pads and no hooves," said Albert. "And there are more strange pawprints in the park."

"I'd better fetch Sergeant Bumble," said Tiggs.

He bounded upstairs and knocked on his bedroom door. "Wake up, Sergeant Bumble!" he called.

The door opened and Bumble's
sleepy head appeared.
"What's all the noise?"
he asked grumpily.

"Albert's found a strange pawprint in the snow. The thing that made it has no fur and no pads and no hooves," said Tiggs.

"Then we must have a look at it," said Bumble. "Get dressed, Constable Tiggs, quickly now!"

A few minutes later, the two detectives followed Albert to the first pawprint.

"You're right, Albert," Bumble nodded, studying it closely. "That is very strange."

"What do you think made it?"
asked Albert.

"Something very large," said Bumble. "This is serious! We must tell everyone to stay indoors until we find out who, or what, made this pawprint."

They set off through the snow, knocking on doors and warning the villagers to stay inside.

When at last they had spoken to all of them, they headed back to the police house to search through their Book of Unusual Pawprints.

"Now, let me see," said Bumble.
"Could it be a turtle?"
"No, Sir," said Tiggs. "Turtles have flippers and pointy toes."
"A penguin, perhaps?" asked Bumble.
"Too small," said Tiggs.

"What about an elephant, then?" asked Bumble.

"It could be an elephant!" cried Tiggs excitedly. "They're very big and they haven't got fur or pads or hooves."

"We'll have to go outside and see if we can spot the scoundrel," said Bumble.

It was snowing harder. Every little sound made them jump.

"I'm s-scared," shivered Tiggs.

"No need to be scared, Constable Tiggs. It's my duty to protect my officers as well as the village." When they reached the place outside the park where the pawprint had been, it wasn't there any more.

"It's gone!" exclaimed Bumble.
"The snow must have filled it in,"
explained Tiggs.
"Of course," said Bumble quickly.
"That's just what I was going to say."

The other pawprints had gone as well. Tiggs began to shiver as they searched to see if any new ones had appeared.

"I think we'd better go back into the warm," said Bumble. "If that elephant has any sense it won't come out again today."

They hurried back to the police house, where they sat in front of the fire and warmed their feet.

"It is hard being a detective sometimes," mused Bumble. "While we face great danger, the other villagers can feel safe behind closed doors."

"Do you think we'll find some more pawprints in the morning?" asked Tiggs. "I won't be surprised if we do," said Bumble.